# SCOOBY-DOO!

## BEGINNER MYSTERIES

STONE ARCH BOOKS
a capstone imprint

Published in 2017 by Stone Arch Books, A Capstone Imprint
1710 Roe Crest Drive, North Mankato, Minnesota 56003
www.mycapstone.com

Library of Congress Cataloging-in-Publication Data
Cataloging-in-publication information is on file with the
Library of Congress.
ISBN: 978-1-4965-4767-5 (library binding)
ISBN: 978-1-4965-4775-0 (eBook PDF)


Editorial Credits:
Editor: Alesha Sullivan
Designer: Brann Garvey
Art Director: Nathan Gassman
Media Researcher: Wanda Winch
Production Specialist: Katy LaVigne
Design Elements:
Warner Brothers design elements, 1, 4-8, 106-112
The illustrations in this book were created by Scott Jeralds

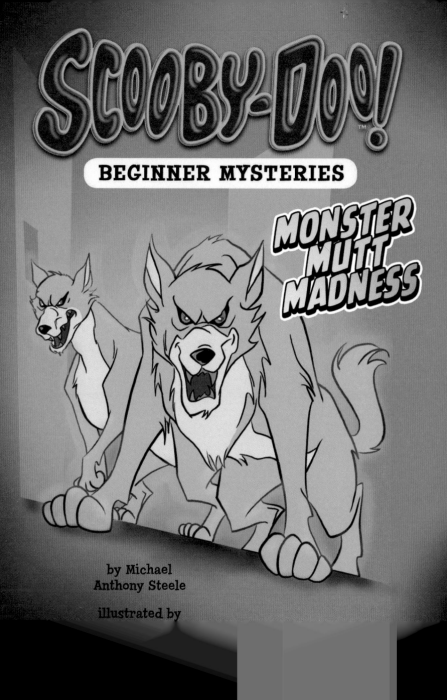

# SCOOBY-DOO!™

## BEGINNER MYSTERIES

# MONSTER MUTT MADNESS

by Michael
Anthony Steele

illustrated by

# TABLE OF CONTENTS

# MEET MYSTERY INC.

## SCOOBY-DOO

SKILLS: Loyal; super snout
BIO: This happy-go-lucky hound avoids scary situations at all costs, but he'll do anything for a Scooby Snack!

# SHAGGY ROGERS

SKILLS: Lucky; healthy appetite
BIO: This laid-back dude would rather look for grub than search for clues, but he usually finds both!

# FRED JONES, JR.

SKILLS: Athletic; charming
BIO: The leader and oldest member of the gang. He's a good sport — and good at them, too!

# DAPHNE BLAKE

SKILLS: Brains; beauty
BIO: As a sixteen-year-old fashion queen, Daphne solves her mysteries in style.

# VELMA DINKLEY

SKILLS: Clever; highly intelligent
BIO: Although she's the youngest member of Mystery Inc., Velma's an old pro at catching crooks.

## CHAPTER ONE

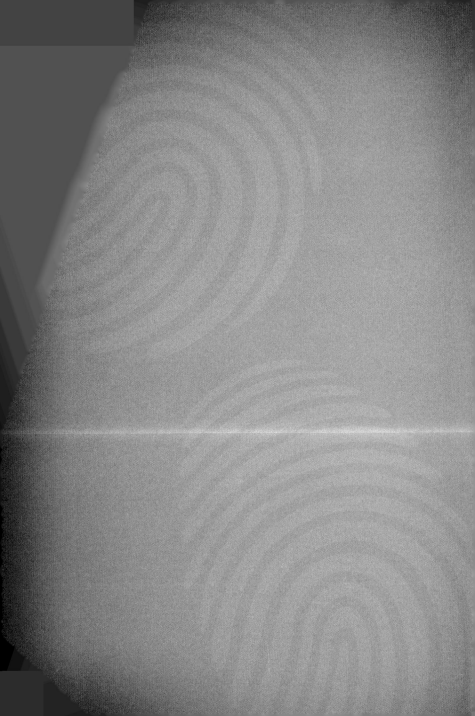

The Mystery Machine pulled
to a stop in front of the *arena*.
The giant building was the location
for many big events like music
concerts, basketball games, and
even monster truck races. Today,
a different kind of gathering was
being held at the arena.

"The Liberty Dog Show," said Shaggy, as he read the large banner over the front entrance. "Like, did somebody enter Scooby in a dog show and not tell me?"

"Robody told me, reither," said Scooby-Doo.

"Don't worry, Scooby," said Velma. "This stop is official Mystery Inc. business."

"That's right," agreed Fred. "We've been asked to check out the strange things that have been happening at this dog show."

"Mrs. Edna Jamison runs the show and she invited us," added Daphne.

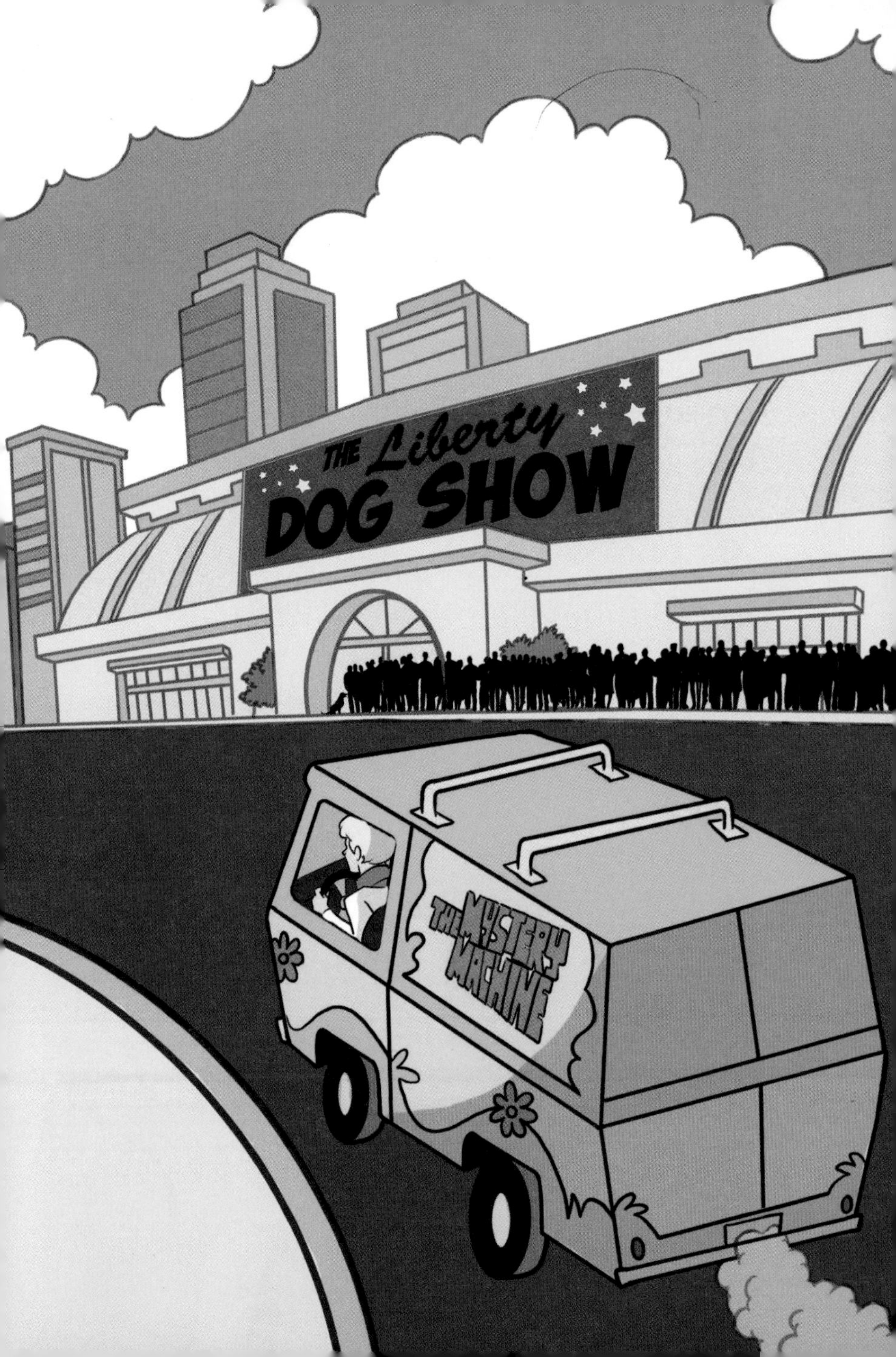
THE Liberty
DOG SHOW
THE MYSTERY MACHINE

Daphne pointed out the van window. "I think that's her now."

The gang climbed out of the van and joined the woman on the sidewalk.

"Mrs. Jamison?" asked Fred. "We're Mystery Inc., and we hear that you have a problem with ..."

Mrs. Jamison held a finger up to her lips. "Shhh," she shushed.

Fred looked at the rest of
the gang.

"We're just here to help with…"
Velma began.

"Shh!" Mrs. Jamison shushed
again.

"Why…" began Daphne.

"Shh!"

"Do we…" added Shaggy.

"Shh!"

"Have to…" added Fred.

"Shh!"

"Be quiet?" finished Velma.

Mrs. Jamison looked around. She
leaned in close to the kids.

"I don't want the others to know I asked you to come," Mrs. Jamison explained. "And dogs have very good hearing, you know."

Scooby nodded.

Mrs. Jamison waved the gang forward. "Come with me, please," she whispered.

The woman led the gang to a side entrance. Once inside the large building, they followed her through a maze of hallways. She showed them into a small office and shut the door. The room was filled with file cabinets. Framed photos of dogs covered the walls.

"There," said Mrs. Jamison. She plopped down in a chair behind a large desk. "Sorry about that, but I wanted to keep your visit a secret."

"Why?" asked Velma.

Mrs. Jamison sighed. "It's the last day of the dog show, and we've had so many people leave already. We've even lost one of the judges." She leaned forward. "Something very spooky is scaring everyone away."

"Don't worry, Mrs. Jamison," said Fred. "We'll get to the bottom of this mystery."

Velma smiled. "It's what we do."

"What's scaring everyone away?" asked Daphne.

"For starters, there are these ghostly *howls*," replied Mrs. Jamison.

"Isn't that normal?" asked Daphne. "After all, this is a dog show."

"And some dogs do like to howl," added Velma.

Mrs. Jamison shook her head. "These howls are not coming from any of the dogs in the show. To be honest, they sound like they are coming from some kind of … monster."

Shaggy gulped. "Like, maybe Scoob and I can go move the van," he suggested. "Maybe to Canada?"

Scooby nodded. "Reah, reah!"

"No way, Shaggy," said Fred. "I have a plan, and you two are going to be key players."

"Ah, come on, Fred," said Shaggy. "Like, just once I'd like to watch one of your plans in action … from a safe distance."

"Don't worry. I'm not asking you to be *bait* for a trap," said Fred. "I want you to pretend to be part of the dog show."

"There are plenty of spots open!" said Mrs. Jamison.

"And I can take the place of your missing judge," suggested Daphne.

"Good idea," agreed Mrs. Jamison. "Thank you."

"Meanwhile, Fred and I can snoop around to see who is trying to scare everyone off," said Velma.

"Before you start snooping, you better look at this." Mrs. Jamison picked up a photo from her desk and handed it to Fred. "This was taken from one of our security cameras."

The gang gathered around Fred to look at the photo. It showed a blurry image of a man running from two strange creatures. The beasts looked like large dogs, but they had glowing red eyes with long, stringy hair.

Shaggy gulped. "I liked it better when it was just a creepy howl."

## CHAPTER TWO

# UNDERCOVER

Shaggy and Scooby-Doo walked into the large *grooming* area. There were rows of tables where dogs were being brushed, shampooed, and blow-dried. Some dogs rested inside large kennels. Scooby-Doo jumped onto an empty table.

"Getting him ready for the big show?" someone asked.

Shaggy looked up to see a man and woman standing nearby. A small, white dog stood on their table.

"Uh, yeah," replied Shaggy. "I'm Shaggy, and this is Scooby-Doo."

"I'm Rick, and this is my wife Ellen," said the man.

Ellen pointed to the dog on the table. "And this is Boomer."

When Boomer heard his name, he stood straight up, held his head high, and pointed his tail.

"Wow," said Shaggy. "He's very … pointy."

Rick laughed. "That's his show *pose*. Boomer's very proud of it."

Shaggy nudged Scooby-Doo. "Come on, Scoob. Show them your show pose."

"Huh?" asked Scooby.

Shaggy leaned in and whispered. "We are undercover. Remember, Scoob?"

"Rokay," said Scooby-Doo. He got to his feet and stood on the table. He thought for a moment. Then Scooby-Doo raised his front arms, shut his paws into fists, and flexed.

"That's ... different," said Ellen.

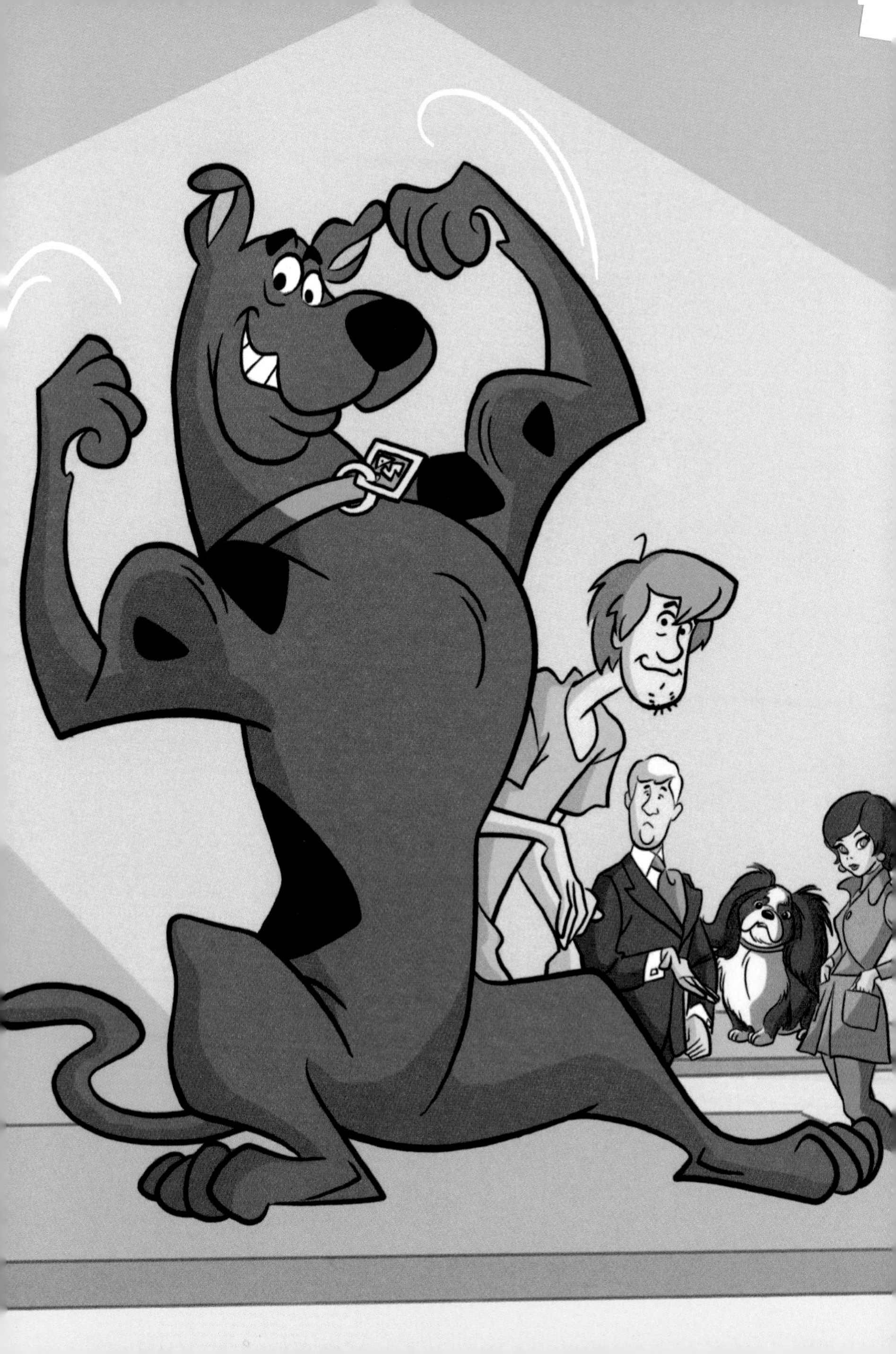

Rick pointed across the large area. "Look! There he is!"

Scooby relaxed as he and Shaggy saw where Rick pointed. In walked a woman with a large poodle.

The poodle's curly, white fur was shaved so it looked as if he had large white cotton balls all over his body.

"That's Joslyn LeRue with her poodle, Percival," explained Ellen. "Percival has won the Liberty Dog Show for the past four years."

Rick turned back to Boomer. He began to brush the little dog. "It's going to be tough to beat him."

Shaggy picked up a brush. "Uh, yeah. Right." He brushed Scooby's back.

"Hee-hee-hee-hee-hee!" Scooby giggled. "Rat rickles!"

Shaggy continued to brush Scooby-Doo. Then Scooby stopped giggling and raised an ear. "Who's ristling?" he asked.

Shaggy looked around. "I don't hear anyone whistling."

All of the other dogs looked around. They heard something too.

"All dogs please make your way to the main judging area," said a woman's voice over the loud speakers.

All of the owners walked their dogs out of the grooming area. Shaggy and Scooby were the only ones left in the room.

"Like, I heard that," said Shaggy. "Were you talking about that woman's voice?"

"Uh-uh." Scooby shook his head. "It was a ristle."

*HOOOOOOOOOOOOOOWLLLLL!*

A ghostly howl filled the air.

Shaggy's legs began to shake. "You sure it wasn't a spooky howl? Because I just heard one."

Just then, the door burst open, and two large creatures came crashing into the room. They each had glowing red eyes and were covered with long, stringy fur.

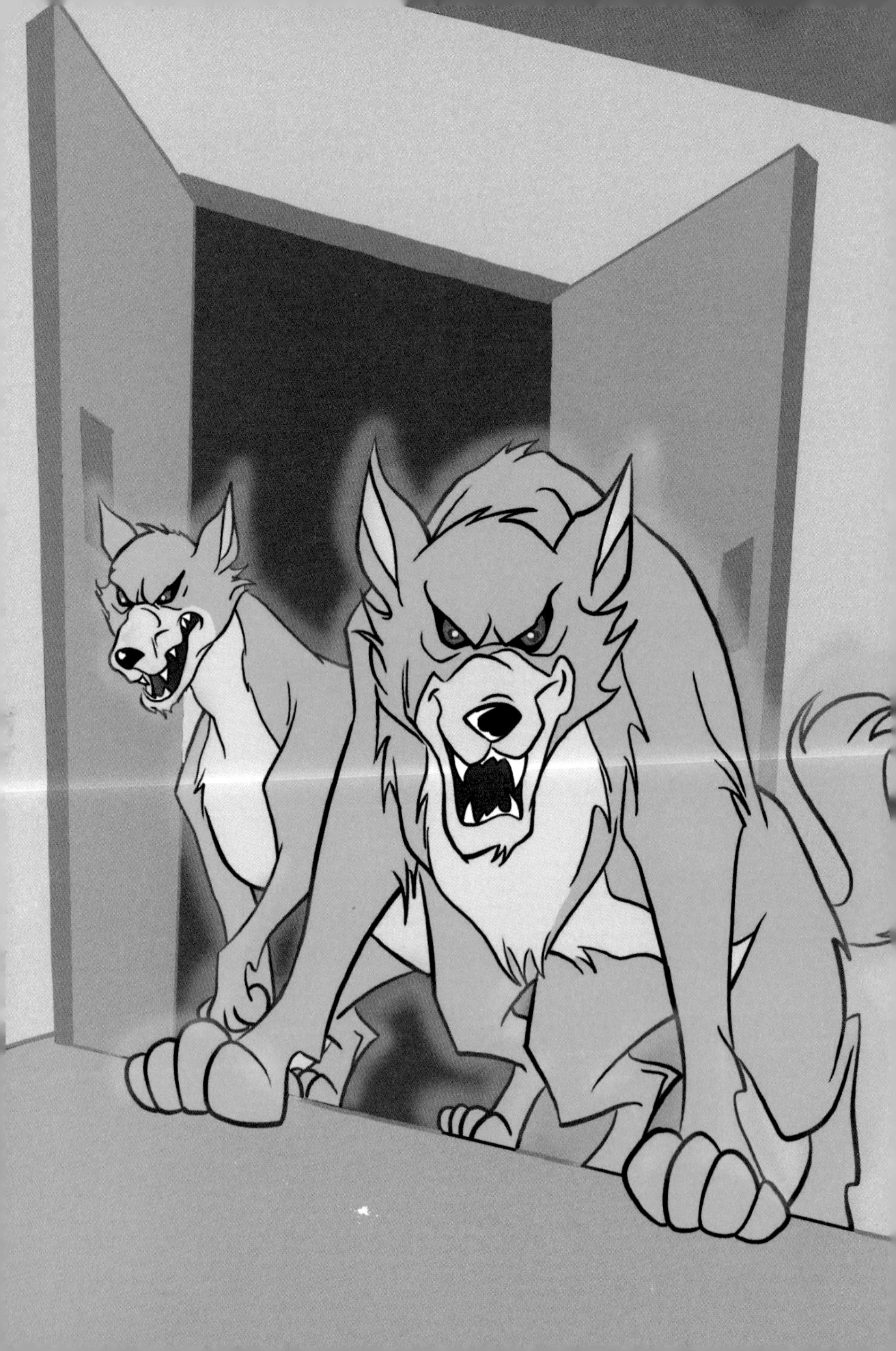

They growled, showing mouths full of large teeth.

"Like, it's the monster mutts from the picture!" yelled Shaggy.

Scooby-Doo and Shaggy were frozen in fear as the animals moved closer.

"Like, I have an idea, Scoob," said Shaggy.

"Rhat, Raggy?" asked Scooby.

"Run!"

## CHAPTER THREE

# BE BRAVE

Fred and Velma walked through the *vendor* area. People were selling all kinds of dog products, from collars to costumes to squeaky toys.

"Do you think any of these vendors would want to close down the show?" asked Fred.

"I don't see why," replied Velma. "They seem to be making a lot of money from all the dog owners."

Fred and Velma went up to a vendor selling small, silver tubes.

"Having trouble training your dog?" a man asked. "If so, then why not try a dog whistle. It's a whistle only dogs can hear." The man blew into the little silver tube, but no sound came out. A nearby dog turned its head to look up at the man.

"That's neat," said Velma. "But we don't need a dog whistle for Scooby-Doo."

"All we need are boxes of Scooby Snacks," added Fred.

Fred and Velma walked by more tables. They saw dog brushes, dog beds, and dog treats. One stand had a small crowd in front of it.

"Is your dog scared of thunder?" asked a man. "Or the vet? Or the mailman?" He held up a small cardboard box. The box had a picture of a dog wearing a cape like a superhero.

"Well then you need a box of Spunky Snacks! The treat that's guaranteed to turn your dog from a scaredy-cat to a brave dog!"

Fred looked at Velma. "Maybe Scooby could use a box of those."

Just then the door at the other side of the vendor area flew open. Shaggy and Scooby raced through.

"Like, look out!" shouted Shaggy. "Crazy monster dogs on the loose!"

Shaggy and Scooby-Doo dove headfirst into a box full of fluffy dog toys. Toy animals and white stuffing flew everywhere.

Fred and Velma looked at the open doorway.

"I don't see anything," said Velma.

Velma and Fred marched over to the giant pile of stuffed toys. They began pulling away the stuffed animals.

They uncovered Shaggy and Scooby who stared straight ahead without blinking. They were trying to blend in with the other stuffed animals.

"You can drop the act, guys," said Fred.

Shaggy and Scooby-Doo looked at each other.

"Are they gone?" asked Shaggy.

"There's nothing chasing you," replied Velma.

Shaggy and Scooby climbed out of the box.

"Phew," said Shaggy. "Looks like we lost them, buddy."

"Lost who?" asked Velma.

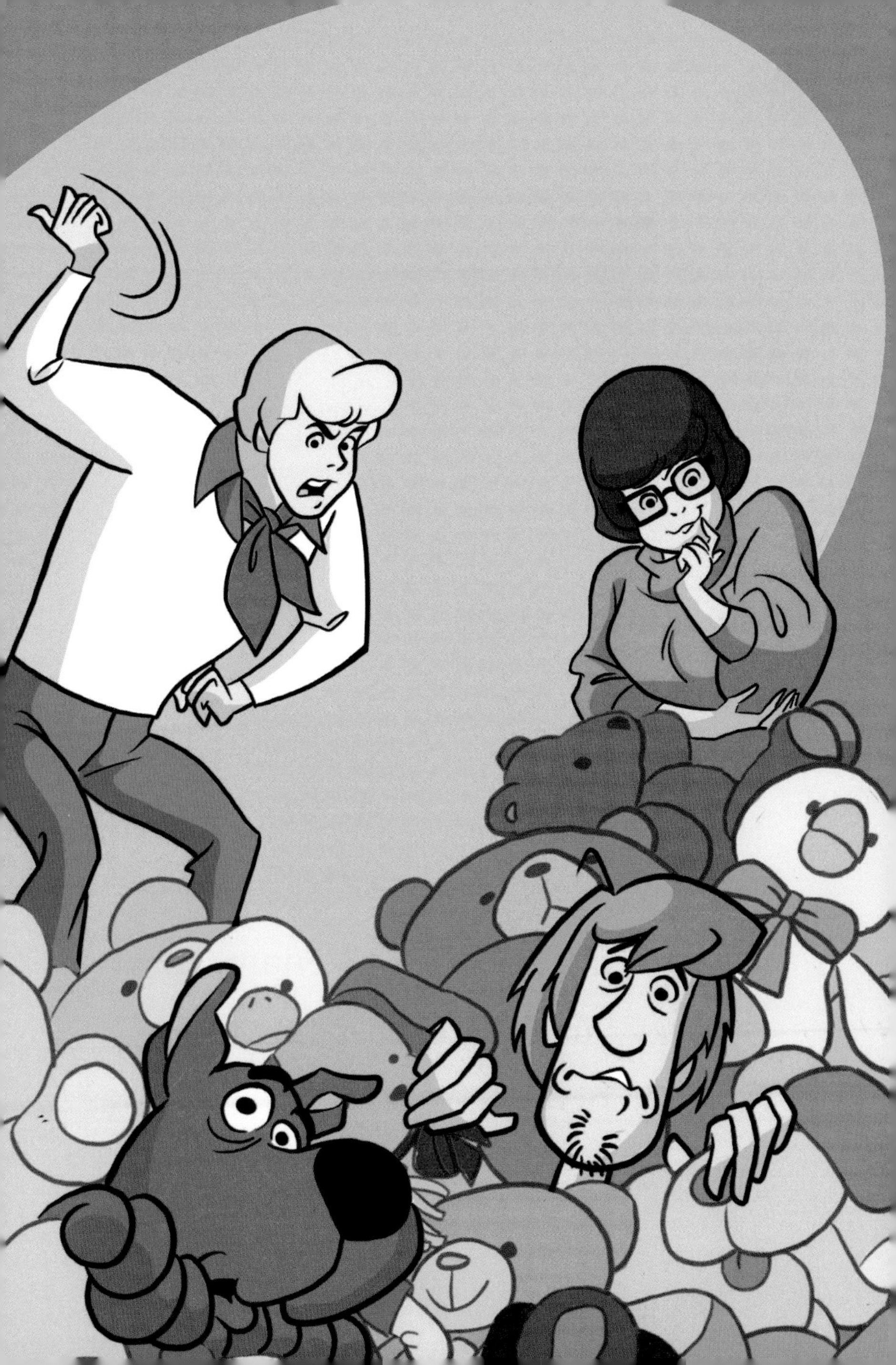

"Like, the monster mutts from the picture," replied Shaggy. "They had big teeth, glowing red eyes, and shaggy fur."

"Rhey were rary!" said Scooby-Doo.

"Sounds like your dog could use a little bravery," said a voice beside them.

Everyone turned to see the salesman they saw earlier. He tipped his hat.

"Alfred Vittman is the name, and Spunky Snacks are my game." He held up his box of snacks.

"Made will all-natural *ingredients*, these tasty treats will make any dog brave as can be."

He reached into the box and pulled out a snack. He tossed it at Scooby-Doo. The dog caught the treat and gobbled it in one bite.

Scooby's ears perked up as he chewed. "Ooh! Rummy!"

"What do you think, Scoob?" asked Shaggy. "Do you feel any braver?"

Scooby-Doo looked around. "I rink so."

"Well, that's good," said Velma.

"Because shouldn't you be in the main judging area with all the other dogs?" asked Velma.

"Oh, reah," said Scooby.

Shaggy gulped and pointed to the doors leading to the main arena. "You mean out there? With all of those people watching?" He turned to Mr. Vittman. "How about a Spunky Snack for me too, huh?"

Mr. Vittman looked confused. "Well, son … they're, uh … supposed to be just for dogs."

Velma shook her head. "Just go with it."

"Yeah," agreed Fred. "Shaggy eats Scooby Snacks all the time."

"Well, uh … okay." Mr. Vittman tossed a Spunky Snack toward Shaggy. Shaggy gulped it down.

"Like, thanks, Mr. Vittman," said Shaggy. He and Scooby ran toward the doorway. "I feel braver already!"

# CHAPTER FOUR

# SHOW POSE

Daphne followed the other two
judges, Mr. Williams and Mrs.
Kavner, as they looked over each
dog. All around them, the audience
watched. Daphne and the judges
were almost finished going down
the long line of different kinds
of dogs.

"Here we have a Scottish Terrier,"
said Mr. Williams.

The older man approached a small gray dog. He stroked the dog's fur and felt his legs. "Shiny coat. Good muscles."

Mrs. Kavner leaned in and marked down something on a notepad. "Good form," the older woman said.

Daphne felt as if she had to say something. "Um ... and his blue collar really brings out the color of his eyes."

The judges turned and stared at Daphne.

Just then, she saw Shaggy and Scooby enter the judging area. They fell into place at the end of the long line of dogs.

Meanwhile, the other judges moved on to the next dog. A large dog stood on the floor next to his owner.

Mrs. Kavner looked at her notebook. "German Shepherd." She and Mr. Williams began to check out the dog like the others.

Daphne reached down and stroked the dog's fur. "Wow. His coat is so soft." She looked up at the dog's owner. "What kind of shampoo do you use?"

The young man looked confused. "Uh ... Pup-So-Soft," he said.

Daphne ran a hand through her own hair. "I may have to try that one myself." She made a mark in her own notebook. "Extra points for using good hair products."

The other two judges stared at Daphne again.

Daphne followed them as they moved toward Shaggy and Scooby-Doo. Scooby sat on the floor and scratched himself behind one ear.

"Oh, my," said Mrs. Kavner. " And here we have a ... Great Dane? I think."

"Like, yeah," said Shaggy. He nudged Scooby-Doo. "Give them your show pose, buddy."

Scooby-Doo stood on his hind legs and flexed his muscles.

"Very unusual," said Mr. Williams.

"Not that one," said Shaggy. "The one Boomer showed you."

"Roh, reah," said Scooby. He stood on all four paws and raised his head high. He poked his tail straight out behind him.

"Much better," said Mrs. Kavner. She reached in to feel Scooby's front leg. "Good muscles ..."

"Hee-hee-hee-hee-hee-hee!" Scooby giggled.

"What are you doing, Scooby?" whispered Daphne.

Scooby flopped onto his back and giggled some more. "Rat rickles!"

Mr. Williams shook his head and made a mark on his notepad.

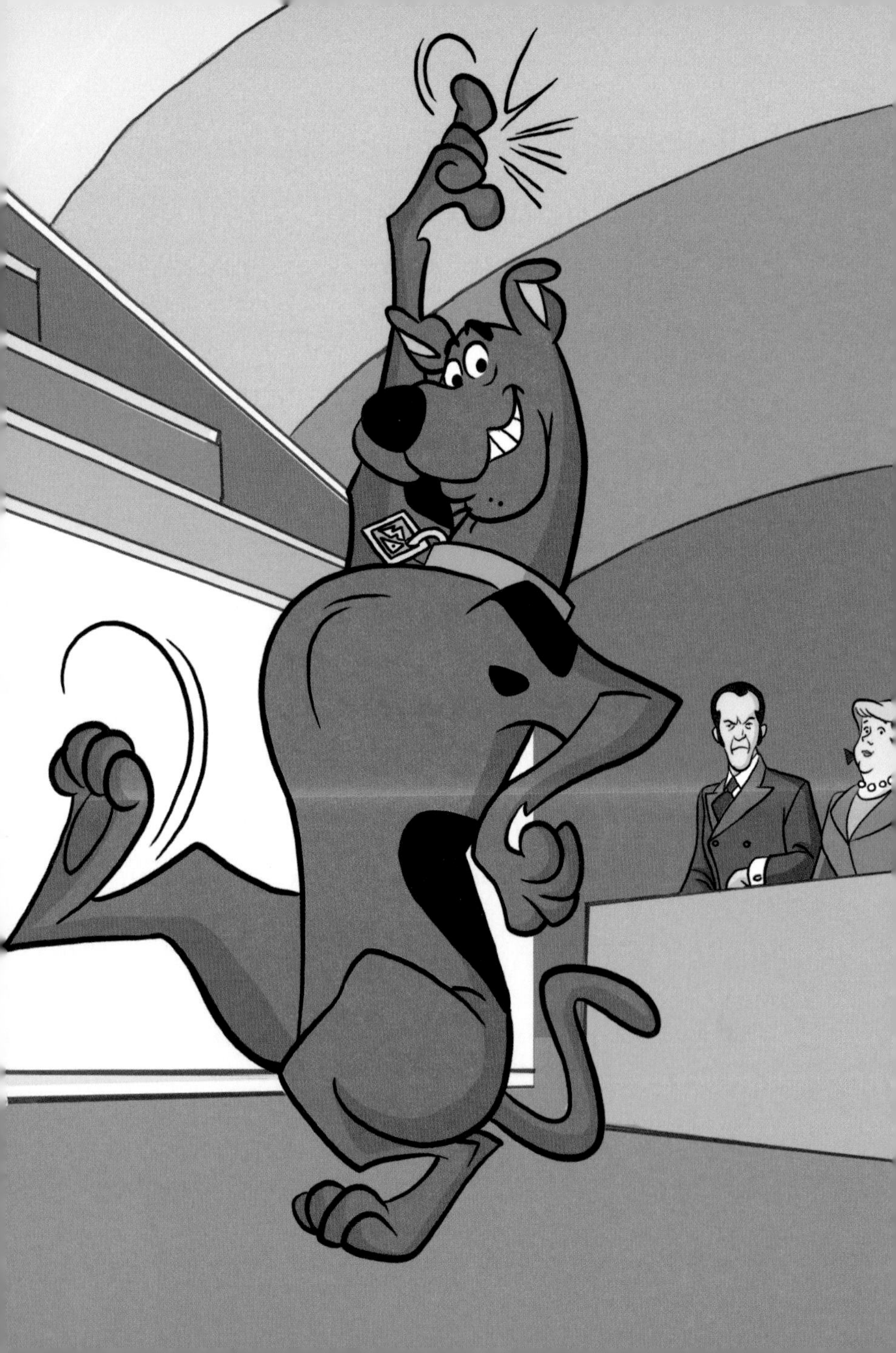

"Like, is there a talent part of this show?" asked Shaggy. "Because Scooby here does a great cha-cha dance."

"Reah!" shouted Scooby. He jumped up on two feet and began to dance. "Run, Roo, cha-cha-cha!"

"Save it for the *agility* part of the show," said Mrs. Kavner.

"What's that?" asked Shaggy.

"That's where we see how quickly and easily dogs run through a special obstacle course," explained the woman.

As the two older judges walked away, one of Scooby's ears popped up. He heard the whistle again.

"Risten, Raggy," said Scooby. "A rhistle."

"I don't hear a whistle," said Daphne.

*HOOOOOOOOOOOOOOOWLLLLL!*

An eerie howl filled the air. The dogs, their owners, and the entire audience looked around, frightened.

"I'll try to keep everyone calm," said Daphne. "You two find out what's happening."

"You can count on us," said Shaggy. "After all, we just had Spunky Snacks!"

Shaggy and Scooby ran across the arena floor to a side door. They pushed through and found themselves in one of the halls. They also found themselves face-to-face with the two monster mutts.

*Grrrrrrrrrrrrrr!*

The spooky dogs growled at them and stared with glowing red eyes.

Shaggy gulped. "Like, I think we are going to need a lot more Spunky Snacks!"

## CHAPTER FIVE

#

Scooby-Doo and Shaggy hugged each other as the monster mutts moved closer. Both beasts growled louder as they crept closer to Scooby and Shaggy.

*Grrrr! Grrrrrrrrrrrrrr!*

"Like, this is the end of a beautiful friendship, huh pal?" asked Shaggy.

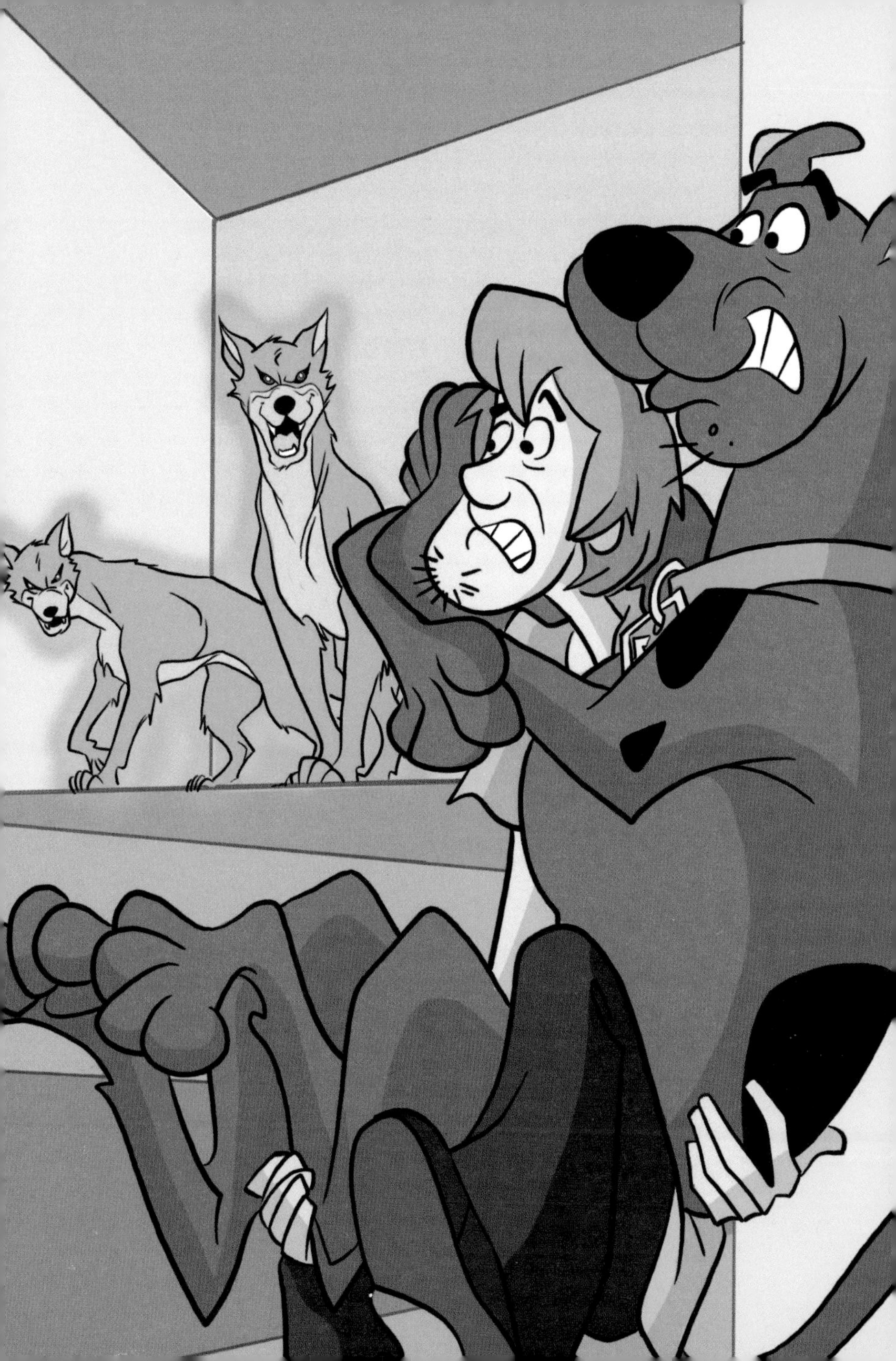

"Reah," replied Scooby-Doo.
"Roodbye, Raggy."

"Goodbye, Scoob," said Shaggy.
The two friends hugged each
other tight. They shut their eyes.

Scooby-Doo's ear popped up. He
heard the strange whistle again.

He opened one eye and saw that the monster mutts heard it too. They stopped growling and looked around. The mutts sped off down the hallway.

Shaggy still hugged Scooby tight. "I'm going to miss all of our good times, Scoob."

"Raggy!" Scooby gave Shaggy a shake. "Rhey're gone."

One of Shaggy's eyes popped open. He looked around. "Oh, yeah. They're gone!"

Scooby spotted a small white piece of fuzz slowly falling to the ground left behind by the mutts.

Scooby pointed to it. "They reft a rue!"

Shaggy picked up the small ball of fluff. "I don't think that's a clue, pal. That's just stuffing from the dog toys. Man, this stuff gets everywhere." He dropped the fuzz ball. "Like, let's find Fred and Velma and tell them what happened."

"Ro-kay," agreed Scooby.

The two ran through the door leading to the vendor area.

"Like, we just had another run-in with those monster mutts," reported Shaggy.

"Reah," agreed Scooby. "Rig and rary!"

"We heard a spooky howl," said Fred. "But we still haven't seen the monsters."

Velma pointed to the Spunky Snacks booth. "I wonder if Mr. Vittman is behind it all."

"Like, why's that?" asked Shaggy.

"Because he's selling a dog treat that is supposed to make dogs braver," replied Velma. "What better way to sell your product than to make everyone scared."

"I don't know how he's doing it," said Fred. "Mr. Vittman has been here the entire time. And he's been selling a lot of Spunky Snacks."

"Boy, I could sure go for some of those right now," said Shaggy. "Those monster mutts were real scary."

Fred handed Shaggy a box. "Don't worry. I got you some."

"Boy, oh boy!" shouted Shaggy. He shook out two snacks from the box and tossed them into the air. Both he and Scooby gobbled one down.

"Mmm-mmm!" said Scooby-Doo, licking his lips.

Just then, Daphne ran up to Shaggy and Scooby. "Where have you two been?" she asked.

"Like, we were just being cornered by two monster mutts," replied Shaggy. He felt braver already. "No big deal, really."

Daphne grabbed each of them by the arm. "Well, you're going to miss the agility part of the show. Come on!" She dragged them back to the main arena.

Velma turned to Fred. "I say we try to spot these monster mutts for ourselves."

"Good idea," agreed Fred.

*HOOOOOOOOOOOOOOWLLLLL!*

Just then another ghostly howl filled the air.

Everyone in the vendor area looked around in fear. A few dog owners grabbed their dogs and hurried for the exit.

"We better get to the bottom of this," said Fred. "Before there are no dogs left in this show."

## CHAPTER SIX

# BALANCING ACT

Fred and Velma explored the halls around the main arena.

"This place is huge," said Fred. "We might be searching for days before we see anything unusual."

*HOOOOOOOOOOOOOOWLLLLL!*

"We may not see anything unusual," said Velma. "But we sure can hear it."

Fred and Velma turned a corner and skidded to a stop. Two creatures sat several feet ahead of them. The beasts were covered with long, stringy hair. The creatures' ears perked up as if they heard something. They got to their feet and walked away.

"Let's follow them," whispered Velma.

Fred nodded, and they stepped out from around the corner. They quietly followed the two mutts as they moved down the hallway. Then the mutts turned another corner and disappeared.

Fred and Velma slowed as they reached the turn in the hallway. They stopped and, once again, peeked their heads around the corner.

*Grrrrrrrrrrrrrr!*

Fred and Velma were face-to-face with red, glowing eyes and huge sharp teeth.

"Jinkies!" shouted Velma.

"Come on!" yelled Fred. He grabbed Velma's hand and pulled her away from the corner.

The two ran back down the hallway as the monster mutts chased after them.

"We have to find a place to hide!" said Velma.

Velma flung open a nearby door. She and Fred pushed through and ran up a flight of stairs.

"Don't look now," said Fred. "But those monster mutts are still after us!"

The beasts chased them up
the stairs. Velma pushed through
another door. She skidded to a stop.
She was on a narrow *platform* high
above the arena floor.

Fred ran through the door
and almost fell off the platform.

"Whoa-o-o-o-o!" His feet balanced
just on the edge.

Velma grabbed the back of Fred's shirt and pulled him back.

"Thanks, Velma," said Fred.

"Don't thank me yet," she said. "We still have monster mutts chasing us and we're out of places to run."

"Not quite," said Fred. He pointed to the nearby *catwalks* stretching out across the open space. The narrow, metal walkways crisscrossed each other high above the floor.

"Oh, boy. I'm not a big fan of high places," said Velma.

She ran down one of the thin catwalks. Fred followed her and the walkway wobbled with every step.

The monster mutts chased Fred and Velma out on the limb.

Fred found himself on one catwalk while Velma stood on another across from him. Velma couldn't get away. There was a monster mutt in front of her and one behind her. She was trapped.

"Velma!" shouted Fred. "You'll have to jump to my catwalk!"

Velma looked down, and her knees shook. "Jinkies! I don't know, Fred."

*Grrrrrrrrrrrrr!*

The monster mutts growled as they inched closer to Velma.

"Don't worry," Fred told her. "I'll catch you!"

Just as the monster mutts sprang forward, Velma closed her eyes and jumped toward Fred. The monster mutts slammed into each other.

With outstretched arms, Fred safely caught Velma. She wrapped her arms around his neck and held on tight.

"Don't worry," he said. "I've got you."

Velma opened her eyes. "But who's got you?"

Fred waved his arms, trying to keep his balance. Teetering back and forth, he and Velma fell off the walkway. Fred grabbed a nearby hanging spotlight.

*PTZZZZ!*

Sparks flew everywhere, as Fred held tight to the spotlight. The cord was connected to one of the catwalks. Fred and Velma swung to the side of the arena, moving toward a large glass window.

"*Aaaaaaahhhhhhhh!*"

*CRASH!*

Fred and Velma smashed through the window and tumbled into a small room.

Fred got to his feet. "Are you all right?"

Velma stood and adjusted her glasses. "I think so." She looked around. "Where are we?"

The small room was full of TV screens. The screens showed different rooms all over the arena. They could see people in the vendor area. They saw dogs and their owners competing in the main arena. Some of the screens even showed a few empty hallways.

"This must be the security room," said Velma.

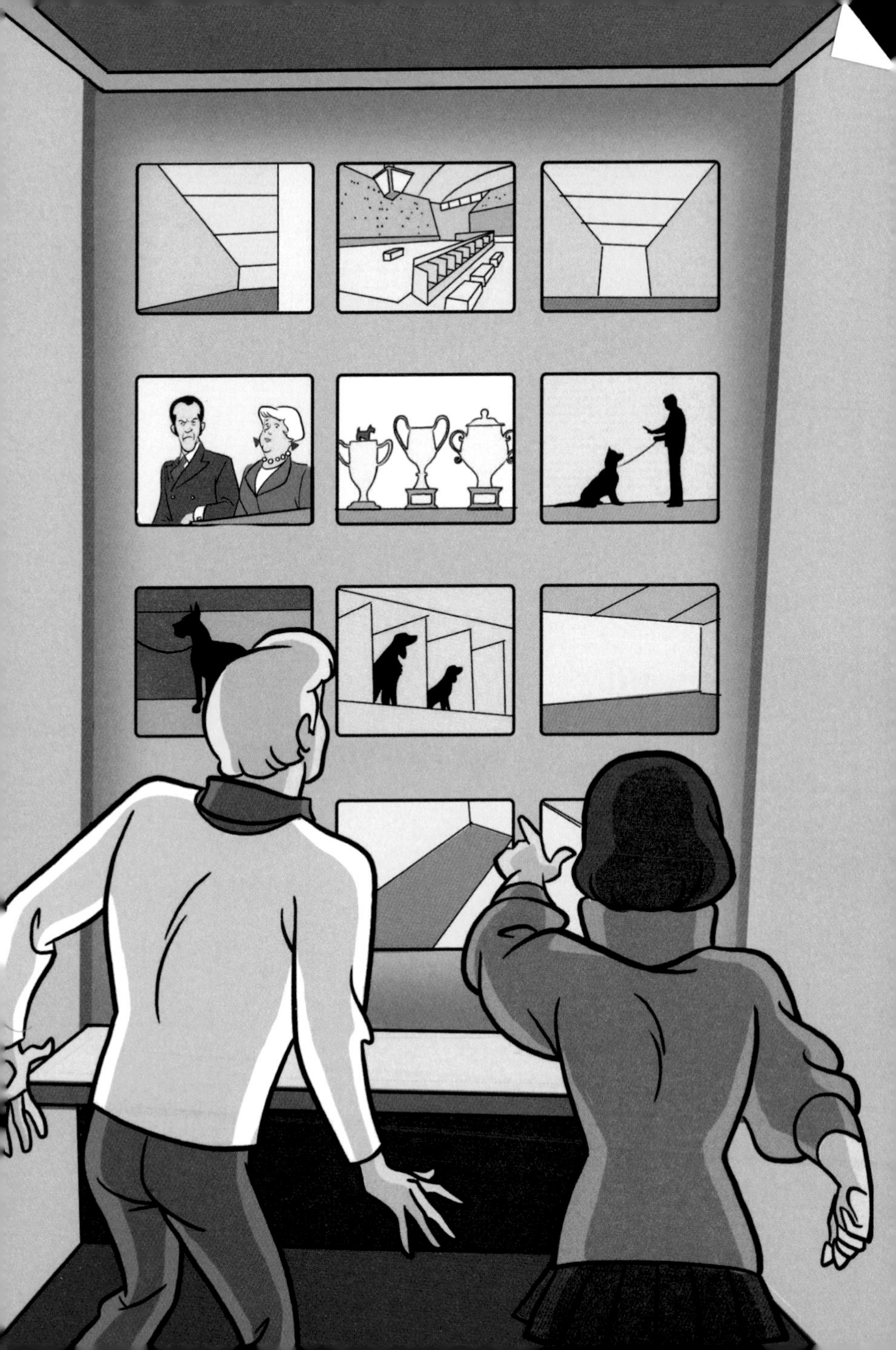

"Check this out." Fred picked up a small silver tube from a desk in the room. "It's one of those dog whistles."

Velma pointed to something else on the desk. "Right next to that microphone." She looked up at the screens. "I bet someone can sit up here and blow the whistle so that it plays through all the speakers in the arena."

"Yeah," agreed Fred. "And watch everything on these screens."

Velma moved toward the door. "I think I know a way to find out who's behind all of this."

As Fred followed Velma, he stopped and picked up something off the floor. "Here's another clue." He held up a piece of white fluff. "Never mind. It's more stuffing from those dog toys. Boy, that stuff gets everywhere."

"Maybe," said Velma. She leaned in to get a better look. "Or maybe it's a clue after all."

## CHAPTER SEVEN

# BIG FINISH

Shaggy and Scooby-Doo were last in line for the agility course. Dogs zigzagged around small posts on the ground and jumped over bars. Shaggy and Scooby watched as dogs ran up and down a tall wooden *ramp.* It was almost Scooby's turn.

"All right, Scoob," said Shaggy. He rubbed Scooby-Doo's shoulders. "You can do this, buddy."

Scooby-Doo looked at the course and all the people watching.

He gulped. "Rat hill is a rittle tall."

Shaggy held up the box of Spunky Snacks. "Don't worry, pal." He reached in and pulled out a handful of treats. "I got you covered."

Over at the judges' table, Daphne motioned to Shaggy that it was Scooby's turn. "And ... go!" said Shaggy.

Scooby-Doo raced across the field. He zigzagged around the posts. Then he dashed up the hill and zipped down the other side.

Scooby-Doo skidded to a stop at the finish line.

"Ra-daaaa!" shouted Scooby-Doo. He bowed as the crowd clapped and cheered.

*HOOOOOOOOOOOOOOOWLLLLL!*

Everyone went quiet in the arena. Daphne ran out onto the field to join Shaggy and Scooby-Doo.

"Did you hear that?" asked Daphne.

"Like, yeah," replied Shaggy. "And it can only mean one thing."

Suddenly, the two monster mutts ran into the arena.

The crowd screamed and began to scatter in every direction. Dogs ran toward the exits.

"Come on, Scoob," said Shaggy. "Like, let's lead those mutts away from all these people!"

"Rood idea," agreed Scooby.

"What?" asked Daphne. "You want those things to chase you? You two?"

"Don't worry, Daph," said Shaggy. "We've been eating Spunky Snacks. They're special treats that make you brave. We're not afraid of anything."

Shaggy turned toward the beasts and began to wave.

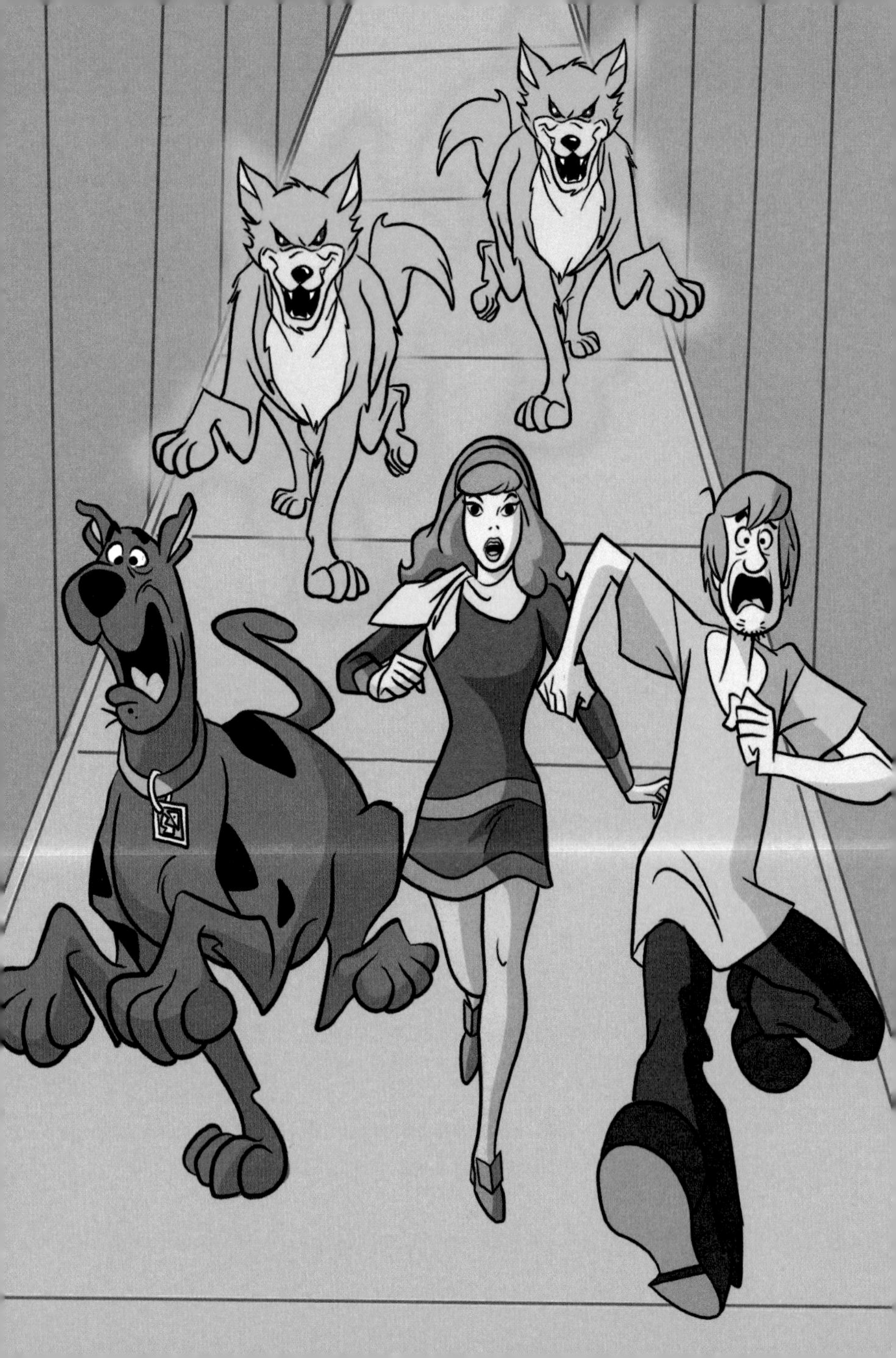

"Yoo-hoo! Creepy monster mutts! Come and get us!" yelled Shaggy.

The two beasts turned their red eyes on Shaggy. They growled and sprang toward him.

"Come on!" shouted Shaggy.

He led the way as Daphne and Scooby followed. The monster mutts were close behind as they headed toward a set of doors.

"Maybe I need a Spunky Snack!" cried Daphne as she ran.

# CHAPTER EIGHT

# THE FINAL CLUE

Shaggy, Scooby, and Daphne raced through the halls in the arena. They sprinted up and down staircases and through the maze of hallways. No matter how fast they ran, the monster mutts stayed on their tails.

"Like, find a place to hide, Daphne," said Shaggy. "Scoob and I will distract them."

Scooby-Doo nodded. "Reah! Reah!"

"Okay, you two are really starting to freak me out," said Daphne.

"I'm telling you, Daphne, it's the Spunky Snacks," Shaggy explained. "Like, I guess everyone will have to get used to us being brave from now on."

"It's just plain weird," said Daphne, as she turned a corner and looked for a place to hide.

Shaggy and Scooby skidded to a stop in front of a supply closet. They ducked inside. They closed the door just as the monster mutts caught up to them.

The two beasts growled and clawed at the door.

*Grrrrrrrrr! Grrrrr!*

*BAM!*

The door flung open and knocked the mutts across the hall. Shaggy and Scooby leaped out of the supply closet. They each wore a gray uniform. Shaggy held a mop while Scooby-Doo pushed a rolling bucket of soapy water.

"I tell ya, these dog shows sure are tough on us working guys," said Shaggy.

"Rou said it," agreed Scooby.

Shaggy leaned on his mop.
"Like, I've already gone through
two pooper-scoopers."

The monster mutts got to their feet. They lowered their heads and growled at Shaggy and Scooby. They stared at them with blazing red eyes.

Shaggy looked up.

"Hey! You're tracking dirt all over our clean floors!"

The monster mutts looked ashamed. They lifted their paws and checked the bottom of their feet.

Shaggy bent down to the mop bucket. "Like, I guess we'll have to start all over." He tilted the bucket toward the mutts. Soapy water splashed all over the floor underneath their feet.

"Come on, Scoob!" shouted
Shaggy.

Shaggy and Scooby ripped off
their uniforms and climbed onto the
rolling mop bucket. Scooby paddled
with the mop as they rolled down
the hallway.

The monster mutts looked at each other and then back to Scooby and Shaggy. They grumbled and ran after them. But the floor was too slippery.

At the end of the hallway, Shaggy and Scooby hopped off the bucket. They turned the corner and ran. They found an unlocked door and ducked inside. Suddenly a bright light blinded them.

"Like, who turned on the light?" asked Shaggy.

"Shaggy and Scooby!" said Velma. She lowered her flashlight. "Boy, are we glad to see you!"

Velma, Fred, and Daphne stood in front of an open file cabinet. They were in Mrs. Jamison's office.

"Just in time too," added Daphne. "Fred and Velma found out who is behind the monster mutt mystery."

Shaggy held out his hands. "No, no. Don't tell me," he said. "Like, I don't want to ruin the surprise of Velma's report at the end."

"She's rery good at it," added Scooby.

Velma smiled. "Thank you, Scooby."

"Well, before that can happen," said Fred, "we need to take care of those mutts once and for all."

Shaggy raised his hand. "Ooh! Like, can we be the bait for one of your traps?!!"

"Reah, reah!" agreed Scooby. "Preese say res! Preese say res!"

Fred walked over to Shaggy and Scooby. He looked them square in the eyes. "Who are you, and what have you done with the real Shaggy and Scooby?"

"It's the Spunky Snacks, isn't it?" asked Velma.

"Okay," said Fred. "Here's what we'll do ..."

## CHAPTER NINE

# WHISTLE WHILE YOU WORK

Shaggy and Scooby walked through the grooming area. Many of the dogs and their owners had left the show. But there were still some left getting ready for the next event.

"Like, I hope this works, Scoob," said Shaggy. "Before everyone gets scared and leaves."

"Reah," agreed Scooby-Doo.

Shaggy stopped and looked around. "All right. Here goes nothing."

Shaggy put the silver dog whistle to his lips and blew. All around them, dogs stopped what they were doing.

*HOOOOOOOOOOOOOOWLLLLL!*

The two monster mutts pushed through a nearby door. People in the crowd screamed and ran.

Shaggy held up his hands. "It's all right, folks. Like, they want us, not you." He blew into the whistle once more.

The monster mutts turned toward Shaggy and Scooby. They growled as they crept closer.

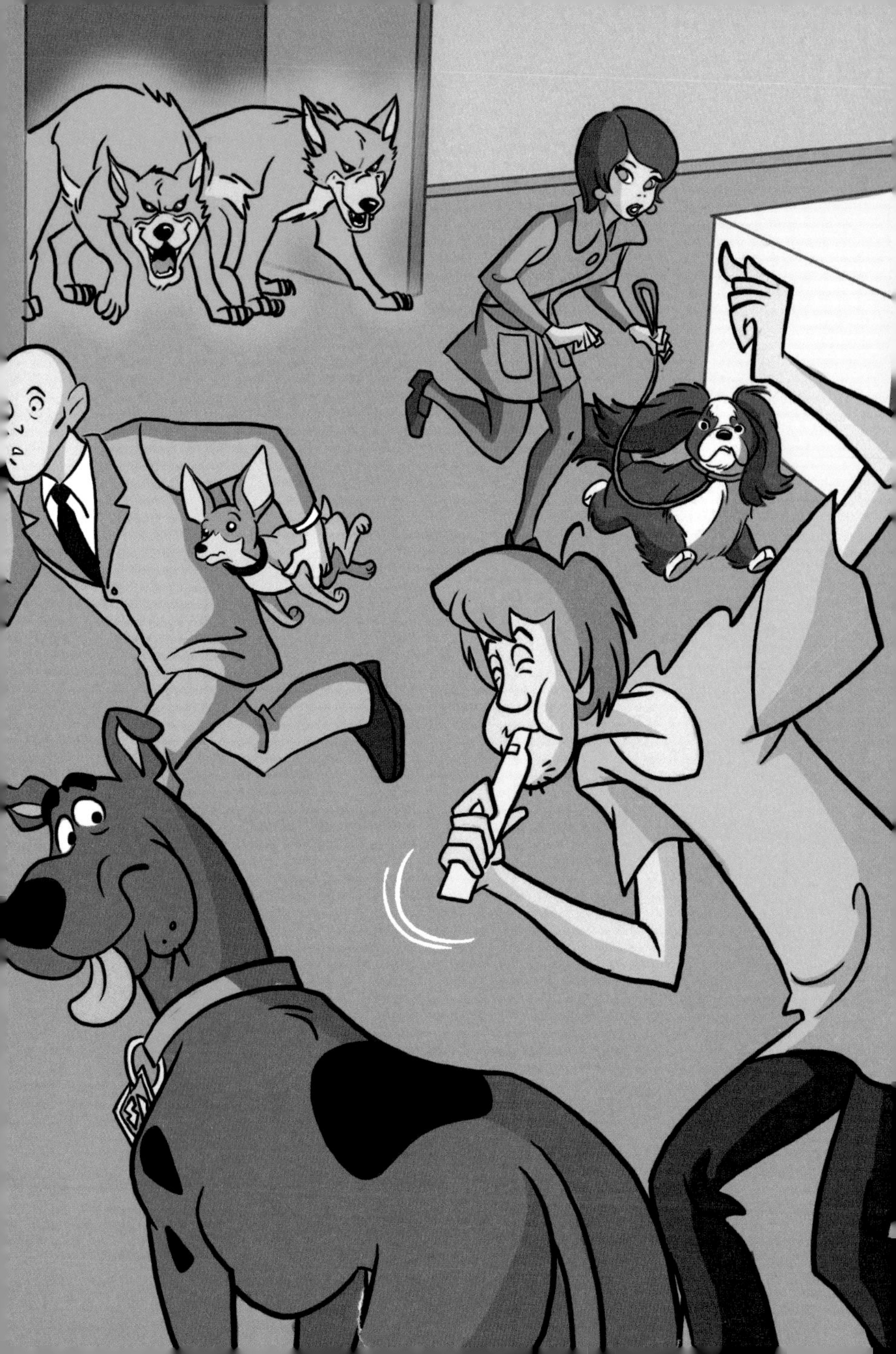

"Now, Scoob!" shouted Shaggy.

He and Scooby-Doo took off. They ran through the grooming area with the monster mutts close behind. They pushed through the door that led to the vendor area.

The big beasts followed. Shaggy and Scooby zigzagged around the booths. The monster mutts were about to catch up with them.

Just then, Velma popped out from behind a *costume* booth. She blew her dog whistle, and the mutts skidded to a halt.

They were about to go after her when Fred popped out from behind a grooming supply booth.

He blew a dog whistle, and the mutts turned toward him. Then Daphne came out of hiding and blew her dog whistle too.

The monster mutts looked left to right, up and down, side to side. They didn't know whom to chase.

Scooby-Doo took his position in front of a pile of stuffed animal dog toys. "Rooby-rooby-doo!" he shouted.

Everyone stopped blowing the whistles. The monster mutts locked eyes with Scooby-Doo. The beasts took off after him. Scooby-Doo turned and dove into the pile of stuffed toys.

The monster mutts leapt in
after him.

*BOOF!*

Stuffed dog toys and stuffing flew
everywhere. A cloud of fluffy, white
stuffing filled the air.

Shaggy ran up to the pile. "Like, are you okay, Scoob?"

When the stuffing settled, the pile of toys was gone. Instead, a large cage stood in its place. The monster mutts were supposed to be trapped inside the kennel. Instead, Scooby-Doo was stuck inside. The monster mutts stood on each side of him.

"Ruh-roh," said Scooby-Doo.

*Grrrrrrrrrrr! Grrrr!*

The monster mutts growled as they inched closer to Shaggy.

## CHAPTER TEN

# HOUNDED

"Like, that's it," said Shaggy.

He pointed at the monster mutts.

"Sit!"

The mutts stopped moving. They looked at each other and then back to Shaggy. Then they both … sat down.

Shaggy raised his eyebrows. "Like, that actually worked." He pointed at the mutts again. "Lie down!"

The mutts both lay down.

"Okay, roll over," ordered Shaggy.

The mutts rolled over. Their long tongues drooped from their mouths as they panted happily.

"They don't look so scary now," said Shaggy.

"That's because they're not monsters at all," said Velma.

Velma and Fred walked over to the mutts. They each grabbed the backs of their collars. When they pulled, the mutts' long, shaggy costumes came off. There were two tiny red lights on each costume where their eyes were. When the costumes were gone, all that was left was two big hound dogs.

Daphne opened the kennel for Scooby-Doo. Everyone gathered around Velma and the hounds.

Velma smiled at the crowd. "Now, it's time to reveal who's behind all of this."

"Okay, I did it!" shouted Mr. Vittman. He shook his head as he walked toward them. "I can't keep my secret any longer."

"Mr. Vittman?" asked Daphne. "You were controlling the monster mutts this whole time?"

Mr. Vittman looked confused. "What? No. I don't know anything about that."

"Then what did you do?" asked Fred.

Mr. Vittman sighed. "I made up the whole story about Spunky Snacks. They don't make dogs brave. They are nothing more than tasty dog treats."

"What?" asked Shaggy.

"Rhat?!" asked Scooby-Doo.

"We thought you were behind all this at first," admitted Velma. "But then we found the dog whistle in the security room."

"And we knew then that the monster mutts had to be well-trained dogs," added Fred.

"After checking everyone's files, we discovered that Joslyn LeRue used to be a dog trainer for movies and TV commercials," reported Velma.

Mrs. LeRue looked shocked. "That's true. But why would I want to scare everyone away from the dog show?"

"That doesn't make any sense," said Mrs. Jamison.

"She and Percival have won the Liberty Dog Show for the past four years," he continued.

Shaggy wasn't listening. He stood there with wide eyes. "But … the Spunky Snacks …"

Velma held up a small white fluff ball. "That's where the final clue comes in."

"At first we thought these things were just stuffing from the dog toys," said Fred.

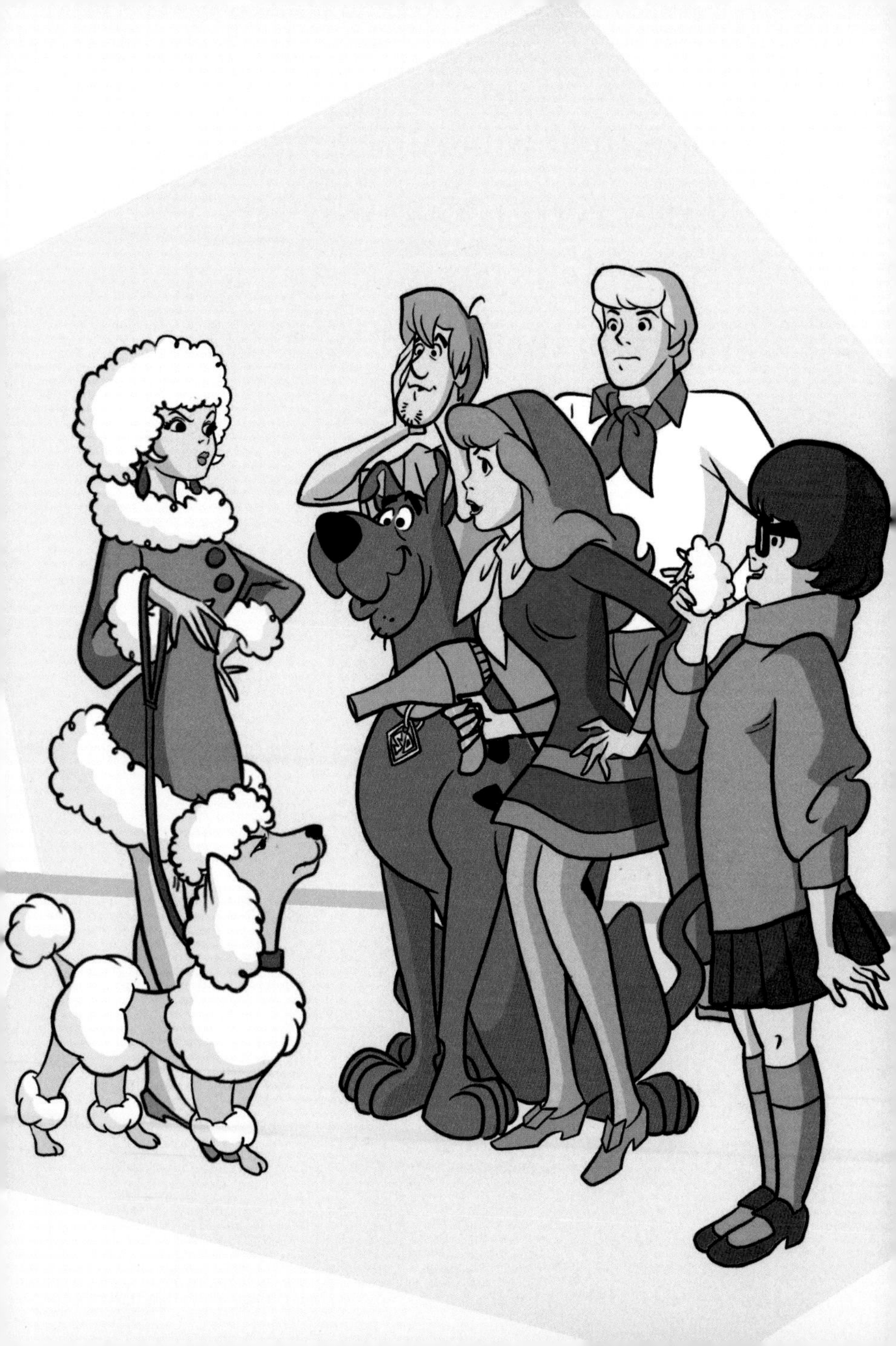

"But then we realized that there is a very good reason why Mrs. LeRue would want to drive everyone away from the show," said Velma. "Hit it, Daphne."

Daphne plugged in a hair dryer from one of the grooming supply booths. She turned it on and aimed it at Percival. When the air hit him, it blew away all his fluffy fur balls. Soon, the dog was completely hairless.

Everyone took a deep breath in surprise.

Shaggy shook his head. "But the Spunky Snacks …"

Mrs. LeRue hung her head as two security guards took her by the arms. "It's true. We tried a new shampoo, and Percival lost his hair. I didn't want the judges to find out about his fake fur."

"But if everyone else left the dog show, you and Percival would win again," finished Velma.

"That's right," agreed Mrs. LeRue. "And I would've gotten away with it, if it weren't for you meddling kids!"

The security guards hauled Mrs. LeRue away.

Shaggy still looked wide-eyed. "But the … Spunky Snacks … aren't real?!!"

Velma walked over to him. "That's right, Shaggy. You were brave all on your own."

"You were great, Shaggy," said Fred. He slapped Shaggy on the back.

*HOOOOOOOOOOOOOOWLLLLL!*

Everyone spun around to see Scooby-Doo sitting between the howling hound dogs. Scooby pointed his nose into the air and joined them.

*"Rooby-rooby-howooooool!"*

## THE END

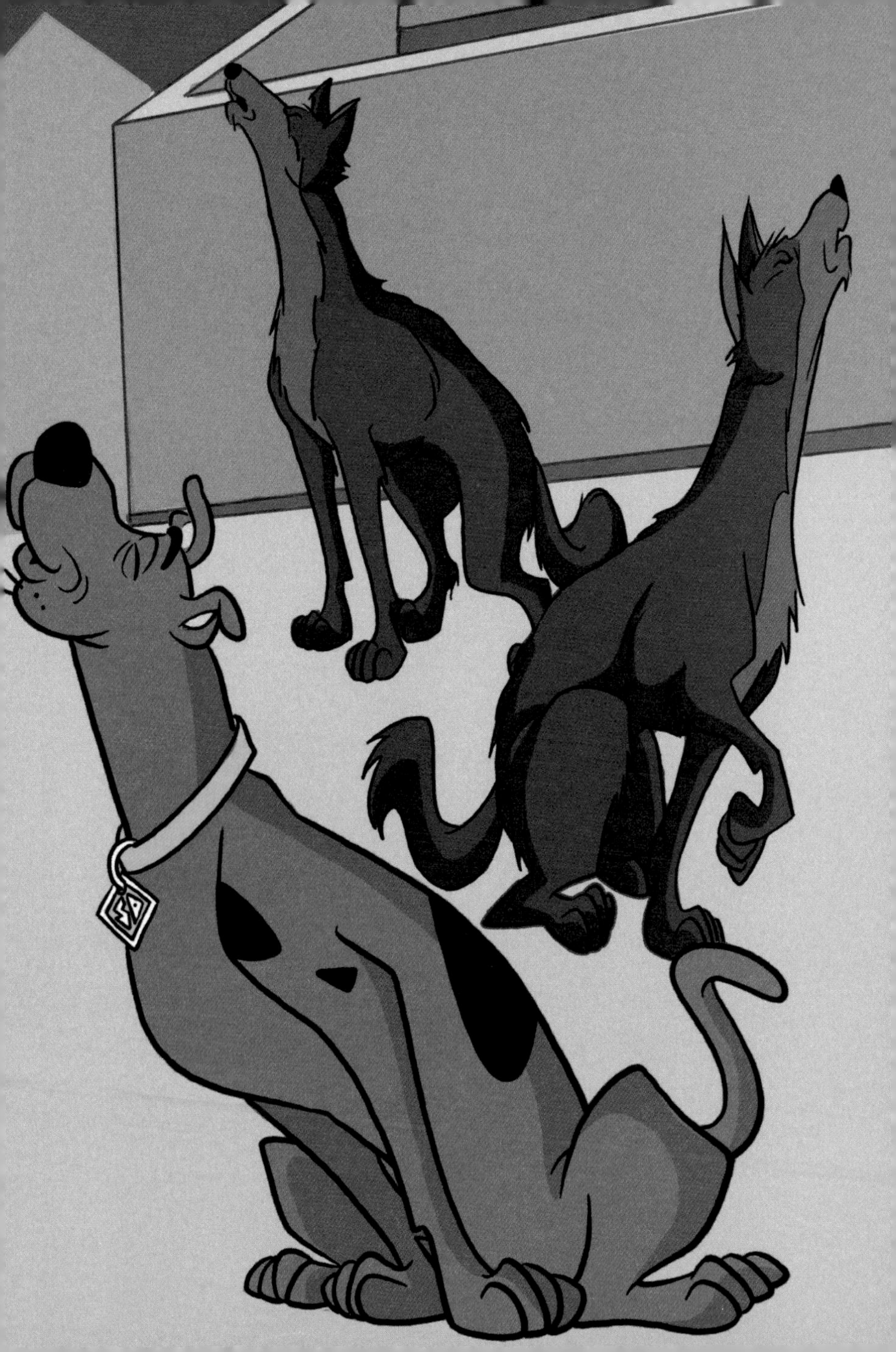

# ABOUT THE AUTHOR

**MICHAEL ANTHONY STEELE** has been in the entertainment industry for more than 24 years writing for television, movies, and video games. He has authored more than one hundred books for exciting characters and brands, including Batman, Green Lantern, Shrek, LEGO City, Spider-Man, Tony Hawk, Word Girl, Garfield, Night at the Museum, and The Penguins of Madagascar. Mr. Steele lives on a ranch in Texas but he enjoys meeting his readers when he visits schools and libraries all over the country. He can be contacted through his website, MichaelAnthonySteele.com

# ABOUT THE ILLUSTRATOR

**SCOTT JERALDS** has created many a smash hit, working in animation for companies including Marvel Studios, Hanna-Barbera Studios, M.G.M. Animation, Warner Bros., and Porchlight Entertainment. Scott has worked on TV series such as *The Flintstones, Yogi Bear, Scooby-Doo, The Jetsons, Krypto the Superdog, Tom and Jerry, The Pink Panther, Superman,* and *Secret Saturdays,* and he directed the cartoon series *Freakazoid,* for which he earned an Emmy Award. In addition, Scott has designed cartoon-related merchandise, licensing art, and artwork for several comic and children's book publications.

# GLOSSARY

**AGILITY** (uh-GI-luh-tee)—a dog sport in which a dog owner directs a dog through an obstacle course in a race for both time and accuracy

**ARENA** (uh-REE-nuh)—a large area that is used for entertainment or sports

**BAIT** (BAYT)—food used as a trap for catching animals

**CATWALK** (kat-WOK)—a narrow walkway high in the air

**COSTUME** (KOSS-toom)—clothes someone wears to hide who he os she is

**GROOMING** (GROO-ming)—cleaning and making an animal look neat

**HOWL** (HOUL)—to make a loud, sad noise

**INGREDIENT** (in-GREE-dee-uhnt)—the different things that go into a mixture

**PLATFORM** (PLAT-form)—a flat, raised structure where people can stand

**POSE** (POHZ)—to keep one's body in a particular position

**RAMP** (RAMP)—a slanted surface that joins two levels

**VENDOR** (VEN-dur)—a person or company offering something for sale

# DISCUSSION QUESTIONS

1. What's your favorite kind of dog? Why is it your favorite? What do you like best about it?

2. Joslyn LeRue tried to cheat to win the dog show. What are some reasons why it is wrong to cheat?

3. Scooby-Doo did some amazing tricks during the dog show. What kind of tricks can you do?

# WRITING PROMPTS

1. Scooby-Doo and Shaggy thought that Spunky Snacks made them brave. But they were brave all on their own! Write about a time when you were brave.

2. The Liberty Dog Show was a fun contest. Come up with your own cool contest, and write about what you would do to win.

3. Scooby-Doo and the gang solve many mysteries and go on all kinds of adventures. Write about what they might do next.

# LOOK FOR MORE

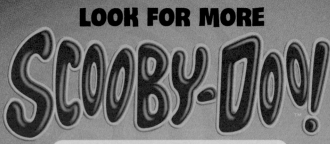

SCOOBY-DOO!

**BEGINNER MYSTERIES**